Civil War Christmas

# *No Tears*
NO
# *for Christmas*

## By Helen Topping Miller

"No Tears for Christmas" is a tale of
how the spirit of Christmas brotherhood
came to an old plantation in Civil War
days. The Confederates were in retreat
in Tennessee. Their armies passed by
the Hunter place, where a sad Christmas
was in prospect. For one of the Hunter
boys had been killed; a second son, badly
wounded, was in the old desolate house.
Then Union troops occupied the plantation. Union soldiers were wounded.
But the spirit of peace on earth, good
will to men triumphed over suffering

*(Continued on back flap)*

for Christmas" on Civil War papers
and diaries.

# NO TEARS
# FOR
# CHRISTMAS

BY

HELEN TOPPING MILLER

LONGMANS, GREEN AND CO.

NEW YORK · LONDON · TORONTO

LONGMANS, GREEN AND CO., INC.
55 FIFTH AVENUE, NEW YORK 3

LONGMANS, GREEN AND CO. LTD.
6 & 7 CLIFFORD STREET, LONDON W 1

LONGMANS, GREEN AND CO.
20 CRANFIELD ROAD, TORONTO 13

NO TEARS FOR CHRISTMAS

PUBLISHED SIMULTANEOUSLY IN THE DOMINION OF CANADA BY
LONGMANS, GREEN AND CO., TORONTO

FIRST EDITION

LIBRARY OF CONGRESS CATALOG CARD NUMBER 54-11441

Printed in the United States of America

# NO TEARS FOR CHRISTMAS

# 1

DECEMBER of 1863 promised a dreary Christmas.

For two years war had darkened the land. Now, in the Tennessee Valley east of Knoxville and Mossy Creek, the tragic depression of defeat lay like a gun-gray cloud, heavy and sour as the wintry sky. General James Longstreet, sent by General Lee, to hold the Union Army of the Cumberland at Knoxville, had been forced into a disastrous retreat.

The proud plantation homes along the eastward route were places filled with fear and trepidation. Slave-owning proprietors were loyal to the Confederacy, and from almost every house a son or brother had gone to fight with the gray-clad armies, at Stone River, at Chickamauga, at the desperately fought-for heights of the Tennessee River, where Sanders of the Blue had fallen.

All around, in the hills and mountains, men were loyal to the Union. Guerrilla forces rode, scattering depredation and terror. Women huddled and waited in fear, while slaves, intoxicated with the new freedom, trailed after the Union troops, or ran away.

The Hunter house stood back on a hill, removed from the highway where the retreating armies beat the half-frozen earth to a chill quagmire.

The house seemed larger than usual this morning because it was so cold.

All the rooms were chilly and in the big hall Teresa could see her breath. Few people lingered in the hall. If they ventured out from the warmth of Mother's room they hurried and slammed doors behind them.

Down the winding well of the stairs an icy draft made the back of Teresa's neck tingle. Or was it a frail sort of excitement because this was Christmas Eve, or was it fear? Teresa knew, though she fought the awareness of it, that they were all afraid lately. Even Mother, though she kept her dread hidden for the children's sake; even Stretch who denied fear hotly. It was because of Davie, upstairs in that frigid attic on a mattress. Probably Davie was scared too.

The younger children, Drusie and Gillespie, assumed a brave attitude when they crept upstairs to crawl back among the cobwebs with little buckets of broth thickened with hominy, inching themselves along over the smoky beams, but the valiant courage forsook them when they scuttled back down again. And today they were all frightened by the endlessly marching men and wagons going by.

Teresa went to stand by the panel of glass beside the wide front door. Presently, Drusie, who was nine, came and plastered her small nose against the glass too, wincing a little from the chill.

"Soldiers!" she sniffed scornfully. "I'm sick of soldiers."

"At least they're still ours," Teresa said with a sigh.

Line on line of them, creaking wagons, stumbling mules, guns lurching through ruts and being dragged out of mudholes. It could have been glory, seeing all those flags and guidons going by, but Teresa knew that this was an end of glory. This was retreat. General James Longstreet's army in retreat before Burnsides' Union forces.

"Dirty," remarked Drusie, letting the curtain fall and turning away, "all covered with mud. Sis, are you going to bake a Christmas cake? Are you? You said you would. Gillespie and I are going to pop corn and string it for the Christmas tree. Lanus promised to cut us a tree. He promised he would."

Teresa ruffled the little girl's hair. "I might as well bake a cake. They'll come. They'll take everything, all the chickens, all the eggs. You can pop corn in Mother's room but don't be noisy and don't fight. Her head aches again."

"She cries too much," said Drusie. "People ought not to cry on Christmas. I hope she won't cry on Christmas."

Teresa went back to the kitchen, Drusie pat-

4

tering after her. The latticed passageway that
separated the brick kitchen from the main house
was bitterly cold; it housed the cistern, the
pump muffled with an old quilt to keep it from
freezing. The kitchen door, greasy with the
patina of many black hands, opened with diffi-
culty. A rolled-up sheepskin had been laid
down behind it to keep out the cold, and the
big, smoky room was hot and dim. Two Negro
women, sitting on stools before the roaring fire,
moved their white eyeballs guardedly.

"Put some coals under the oven, Lizzie," ordered Teresa, "I'm going to bake a Christmas
cake."

The heavier woman grunted to her feet,
"Ain't no vaniller, Miss Tess. Ain't no cinnamon
neither."

"I'll find something." Teresa opened a dark,
cluttered press. It smelled of mice and cloves
and candles. A box of snuff stood close beside
a drying lump of cheese wrapped in a torn rag.
A big china bowl held three eggs and a spool
of black thread. Lizzie was a mess but no one
found fault any more. It was part of the great

pressing uncertainty that lay over everything now, even dreading to antagonize Lizzie.

The thin Negress who had not moved from her stool took a twig she was chewing from her mouth and tossed it into the fire.

"Miss Tess," she said impudently, "Lanus say freedom done come. Lanus say Mist' Linkum say us all free now, ought not to work no more. Lanus say freedom come a long time ago."

Teresa took the eggs out of the bowl, wiped it out with a dismal towel.

"If you don't work, Mir'am, you certainly won't eat. Not here anyway," she snapped. "Get up from there and sift some flour."

"Ain't much to eat noway," grumbled Mir'am, dragging her lank body upright. "Flour bar'l scrapin' bottom now."

"Father will attend to it when he comes home," Teresa spoke with more confidence than she felt. She had to believe in something or this awful winter would be unbearable. She had to believe that Father was able to make things better.

6

Beau was dead. Beau, the handsome elder brother, killed somewhere down near Nashville. Now Mother cried all day long. Father had gone with the mules and wagon to bring Beau's body home. And upstairs under the roof, hidden from the roving Union guerrillas who were continually riding down out of the hostile hill country, lay David, her second brother, with a ragged wound in his thigh.

Lizzie banged shut the iron door of the oven, picked up a pannikin from the hearth. Aromatic steam came from it.

"You take you' Mamma this pennyryle tea, Miss Tess," she said. "I bake the cake. I knows more about bakin' Christmas cake than you does. I ain't studyin' freedom 'round here like some no-count niggers I knows."

"Thank you, Lizzie." Teresa's eyes misted. "It's the children. They should have some kind of Christmas."

On the floor Drusie was thumbing popcorn kernels into a pan. "I'll need a long-handled skillet," she announced, "and some grease—

and some salt. And Lanus had better get that Christmas tree cut before dark."

"Lanus down to the road watchin' them soldiers," snorted Lizzie. "Do he go off wid 'em it don't make no never mind to me. Tote them things in yonder for Miss Baby, you Mir'am. And does you say freedom around Mis'tiss, I smack your jaws good."

Teresa hurried back through the passageway. Every nail was white with frost now, she could hear the wagons squeaking on the frosty road, the soft shuffle of weary feet. The sky was thin and cold and greenish with early night. Soon it would be dark but the tired, thinly clad, hungry men would not dare to halt. They could only huddle briefly around tiny fires, chew parched corn and dried, salty meat, struggle up again to march on. Retreat! Even the word had the sad cadence of a tolling bell.

At the front door she could see the lanterns bobbing under some of the wagons. The hall was growing dark but she did not light the one candle on the table. Candles were getting scarce and precious now, and there was little oil for

8

the lamps. It had to be saved, what little there was for the lanterns used outside. A light would show her the vision of herself in the long mirror, anyway. A girl in a lanky skirt without hoops, shoulders covered with a faded wool shawl. A girl who was eighteen and still pretty, and that was no use at all. Who had time or strength to look at a girl any more, in this ravaged South? With all the young men gone to war, even the older ones, even the boys? She carried the pannikin into the back room where there was warmth and flickering firelight on the wall.

"Lizzie made pennyroyal tea, Mother," she announced. "You're supposed to drink it to cure your head."

The woman in the bed sat up. She was not old, but her thin face had the drained look of age, her eyes were sunken and dark, her thick dark hair curling in disorder around her head.

"Do I have to, Tess?" she sighed. "It will retch me, I'm afraid."

"I'll wet a cloth in it and bind it on your head. We can't hurt Lizzie's feelings. She's up-

set anyway. Lanus and Mir'am are talking freedom and she's afraid Lanus will run off with
the soldiers when the Yankee army comes
through. She's baking the children a cake."

Sarah Hunter moved her hand weakly over
her forehead, pushing back her hair. "The
army? I can still hear them. They're retreating,
aren't they? Sheldon wouldn't tell me, but I
know they are going east. They wouldn't be
going east unless it was a retreat."

On the floor Drusie and ten-year-old Gillespie
had been arguing in whispers, while Gillespie
pushed a long-handled skillet over the coals.
Drusie looked up.

"Gillie says we won't have any Christmas.
We will too, won't we, Mother?"

From the big four-poster the soft voice answered, wearily, "Christ is born, Drusie, and
the angels will sing in the sky, even if we can't
hear them. It will still be Christmas."

Drusie shrugged. "I don't want angels. I want
a tree with candles on it."

"Two of those soldiers got a chicken," announced Gillespie. "I told 'em they were mean

10

as the Yanks but they said—no, they weren't, they were just hungry."

"They're all hungry," said their mother sadly, "but Lizzie had better not fry any meat. It would be torment to those poor men to smell frying meat."

"They'd likely bust in here and take it away from us," said Gillespie, dumping a skilletful of popped corn into a dishpan.

Drusie snatched at the handle. "My turn now! My turn now!" she shrilled.

"Quiet, please, Drusie," begged Teresa. "Loud noises hurt Mother's head."

"Are you going to cry on Christmas, Mother?" Drusie asked.

"No. No, I mustn't cry on Christmas. There must be no tears for Christmas—even if our hearts are breaking."

"Davie has been longing for some ham," Teresa said, "but we'd better not cook any tonight."

"It wouldn't be good for him, as long as he has that fever," said his mother. "Poor child— I wish we could bring him down from that

11

awful place! Drusie, sit back! You'll have your petticoat on fire."

"If we brought him down some night-riders would find it out," argued Gillespie, made wise beyond his years by war. "Stretch says they hate all the river-bottom people who own slaves."

"Lie back, Mother, so I can put this towel on your head. Drusie, you may pull the curtains and light one candle. Only one, now," warned Teresa.

Drusie kindled a splinter at the fire, carried it shakily to the high mahogany chest where the candlesticks stood. "I reckon it's mighty dark up where Davie is," she remarked. "Make Stretch go tonight, Mother. Gillie and me get scared."

"You mean *you* get scared," sniffed Gillespie.

"You run mighty fast down those stairs, Mister Smarty!"

"Lanus shall go tonight," Sarah said.

"Lanus is not here, he's down at the road, Lizzie said."

"Gillie, you run down to the road and tell

Lanus to come here, immediately," ordered his mother. "Tell him I want him at once."

The little boy's eyes widened fearfully. Teresa interposed. "There are a lot of rough men going by, Mother. And Lanus is acting biggity, talking freedom. He might not come even if Gillie told him."

"Well, no matter what that man Lincoln said Lanus belongs to me and he will not be free till I set him free," declared Sarah crisply. "Drusie, you go with Gillespie. Take my wool shawl."

"Mother, please don't make them go!" pleaded Teresa. "Wait till Stretch comes back."

"Sheldon"—their mother always gave her third son his proper name in reproving fashion— "went to take the horses back to the woodland." She set her mouth sternly. "We can't let your brother lie up there, cold, sick, and untended."

"Then I'll go. Gillie can carry the lantern. Come along, Gillie."

In the kitchen Lizzie put a warm pone of bread and a small jar of milk in a tin bucket.

"Don't slop it now, Miss Tess. May not have no cow in the morning. May not be no milk for anybody."

The little boy stumping doggedly ahead with the lantern, Teresa climbed two curving flights of stairs to the attic. Fortunately up here there were no windows, no betraying gleam could be shown to the world outside.

Against one wall of the attic stood a huge, empty trunk. With Gillie helping she dragged it away, revealing a small, square hole that gave access to the black, raftered cavern under the roof. Back out of sight on a mattress, her brother David lay wrapped in heavy comforts and Teresa crept cautiously over the timbers to him, while Gillie held the light inside the cubby hole.

David was not yet twenty. A boyish beard lay like pink fuzz on his drained young face; he tried a grin, tried to pull himself up, but sank back weakly.

"Ham?" he whispered.

"Sorry, dear, no ham. We didn't dare fry meat with the army going by. They haven't raided

14

the house yet but they've been at the henhouse, and if they smelled ham cooking it would be more than they could resist. Here's bread and milk. I'll lift your head while you eat it."

"Why didn't Longstreet hold them at Knoxville?" David demanded angrily. "That's what he was sent up here for, to keep Burnsides and Sanders pinned down, to cut the Army of the Cumberland in two. He could have held them."

"Sanders was killed, Davie. Drink your milk. We don't dare stay long. The light might show through the shingles."

"Father back yet?"

"Not yet."

"He'll never find Beau. They were all blown to pieces down there, they buried them in trenches."

Teresa shivered. "He has to try. He had to try for Mother. And you have to get well for Mother too, Davie."

"If they're retreating, the Yanks are behind them, Sis, you know that. They'll take me."

"We won't let them take you, Davie. Sleep now, and don't worry."

15

"Cold," he whimpered.

"When Stretch comes back from hiding the horses I'll send up some hot bricks for your feet. All right, Gillie—be careful with that lantern."

She had eaten sparingly and brought hot tea and bread to her mother, had tucked the children into one feather bed in a cold upper room, Drusie still fretting about a Christmas tree, when Stretch came back. He was sixteen, very tall for his age, which accounted for his nickname, and lately his young face had grown too set and quiet and grim.

He kissed his mother, laid another log on the fire, and stood staring silently into the fire. Teresa felt the prescience of something impending, put her hands to her cheeks and pressed hard as though to ward off what she did not wish to know or hear.

"Are the horses safe, son?" Sarah inquired from her pillow.

"Who knows? I hope so." The boy kept his gaze on the flames. "Dave had his supper?"

16

"Gillie and I carried it up. Lizzie saved some bread for you, too. It's wrapped up, in the ashes. There's milk, too. I'll get it and you can eat it here." Teresa went out, but Stretch followed her, gestured her into the cold, dark dining room where he closed the door. The room was bleak now, the big table no longer draped in heavy linen for a big family and their guests, the sideboard bare, all the silver buried under the manure pile.

Stretch came close to her, spoke low. "We have to get Dave out. We've got to send him with Longstreet. They're moving their wounded in wagons. A major told me they'd set up a hospital somewhere up toward the Virginia line. He said the Yanks were less than twenty miles behind them. They'll be over the creek before daylight, even though these boys burned the bridge. They'll get Dave and he'll die up in one of their stinking prisons if he doesn't die before they get him there. And it would kill Mother. She can't stand much more, Sis."

"What can we do?"

17

"We'll have to carry him down, you and I. We can't trust any of the Negroes. Not with the Union army only a few hours away."

"Oh, no, Stretch! It might kill him, if that wound starts bleeding again—it could be his death and that would kill Mother. After Beau, it would be too much."

"Sis, I tell you they'll be here by daylight at the latest. They'll be all over the place, they'll find him. We've got to do it. Now, before all the wagons get by. Now, while I'm here to help."

"While you're here?" Anguished incredulity made her voice a little shrill. "Stretch—you can't—"

"Hush, you want Mother to hear? I'm going. I'm going with Longstreet. They've got to have every man. I'm going before Father comes. He'd try to stop me. And Mother mustn't know—not till I'm gone."

"They need every man, yes—but you're a boy! You'll leave us all alone," she protested bitterly.

"Father will be here soon. You've got Lanus

18

and the women. First we've got to move Dave.
I'll go down to the road and halt a wagon—ask
them to wait."

"Stretch, I can't bear it! Beau—then Davie—
now you!"

"I could bring some men in to help but
Mother would hear." He ignored her cry. "I'll
ask a couple of fellows to wait outside the
front door with a litter. Get another blanket.
I can carry Dave alone, I think, he's light and
thin now. You fetch the light."

"At least eat something first."

"No time. The wagon train will be past if
we don't hurry. The artillery have already gone
by. Tell Mother something—tell her you're going out to cook supper for me. Then gather up
what food you can find and make a bundle of
it, and fetch a lantern upstairs."

Inch by inch, every move torture, Stretch
dragged the mattress to the cubby opening.
"Quiet, Dave!" he warned in a whisper. "Chew
your lip—hang on, I'll get you out before the
Yanks come and get you."

Teresa knelt on the icy floor, holding the lantern, grateful for the thin warmth of the chimney near to her face. Davie looked so pale, so drained. . . . She watched the blankets that wrapped him anxiously, dreading the sign of a fresh hemorrhage. There had been so much bleeding from that wound already, a little more and Davie would faint, perhaps die wanly in his brother's arms.

"This will hurt now," Stretch warned, when they had Davie out on the attic floor, "I've got to get you on my back. Ease his legs up, Sis. I'll bend over as much as I can and keep my balance. Hang on, Dave. There'll be a litter outside."

Teresa held David's hand tightly, as they moved cautiously down the two flights of stairs. No bleeding, thank Heaven! Davie clutched at her fingers till they hurt but he made no moan. The front door creaked. It had not been opened in a long time. The high steps were frosty, the lantern flame jumped and wavered in the cold gusts of wind, the faces of the men who waited below there in the yard were pinched and gray in the thin light.

Teresa kissed her brothers good-by, fighting for courage, for calm.

"Good-by, Davie. Good-by, Stretch. Stretch, you take care of Davie now and write to Mother, you hear?"

"I will. 'By, Sis. I'd better take this lantern. Tell Mother I had to go."

The wagons rumbled away. Some weary officers jolted past, half asleep in their saddles, more men on foot slogged into sight, lurching as they walked, throwing the weight of their bodies forward like men made of wood. They did not even look toward a girl standing alone in the dark. The wind whipped her hair and her shawl. There were stars, cold in a remote sky. There would be no snow, at least, to add to the misery of those marching men, no snow falling on Davie's white, wistful face, upturned in the back of that jolting wagon.

She could not have borne it if there had been snow.

# 2

TERESA went back to her mother's room and sat for a long time before the dying fire, huddled in a heavy shawl. On the bed her mother was mercifully asleep. In the morning she would have to be told. All her sons—all but little Gillespie. The clock struck midnight and Sarah stirred and lifted herself on an elbow.

"Christmas day!" she exclaimed in a tragic voice. "Christ's day—and where is He? Why has He forsaken us?"

Teresa went to her quickly. "God hasn't forsaken us, Mother. He'll take care of us. All of us."

Davie, in that rocking wagon, crammed in

with a dozen wounded men. Stretch, tramping doggedly along behind, with the weary, weary line of marching men.

"Then it's time He began," stated Sarah. "I can't endure much more. Why aren't you in bed? Run along now and rest. No one knows what lies ahead for us tomorrow. That Longstreet—he should be tarred and feathered."

"He did the best he could. They have so many more men and more guns. They have more food and ammunition—and everything, Stretch says." She tucked herself into her chair again. "I'll just stay here till morning now, Mother, it's so cold upstairs. You go back to sleep."

"We must have something ready for the servants in the morning, Teresa. You know how it will be—'Christmas gift, Mis'tis.' Look in my chest and find something we can give to Lizzie and Mir'am. A petticoat or a chemise for Mir'am—Lizzie's too fat to wear my things. Give her my red shawl. The one with the fringe. She loves fringe. There'll have to be something for

23

Lanus too, one of your father's waistcoats probably will do."

"Lanus may be gone, Mother."

"He'd never dare run away. Even if that creature in Washington did set them free. I haven't set them free. I wish I had something for the children. They count so much on Christmas. Your father promised Gillie a gun but he's too small to have a gun. Drusie can have my yellow beads. She has always wanted them and I'll never wear them any more. I shall wear black now till I die. I shall mourn for my firstborn son as long as I live."

But Teresa was not listening. She was stiffening, hearing sounds. Horses' feet on the drive outside. Father! Had he come back?

She said, "Do you hear horses, Mother?"

"I've been hearing horses all day," Sarah was listless. "Are all the doors bolted?"

"I did it myself. Nobody could possibly break in—and Lizzie has the only other key. She keeps it on a rag hung around her neck. She even sleeps with it on."

She waited near a window. If it were Father

out there he would be shouting by now for Lanus to come and take the mules. There were no shouts, but there were jinglings and clinkings. Then abruptly there came a heavy pounding on the back hall door.

A voice shouted, peremptory and rough. "Open up—the house!"

Sarah sat up, her dark eyes angry and stubborn. "Don't move, Teresa. Don't answer. It's some of those low bushwhackers. They're after David. Somebody has betrayed us—that rascally Lanus, talking about freedom!"

The knocking came again and Teresa winced with every thud. The doors were strong and heavy, but doors had been broken down at other houses. Then footsteps sounded along the wall of the house and Teresa crouched low, waiting for a bullet to crash through a window where inevitably the fire light must show through the silk curtains. But the rap on the glass was metallic, a pistol butt, or a saber.

"Open the door, you Rebels!" yelled a man's voice.

25

Teresa moved quickly to the window, called through the panes.

"Go away! There are only women and children here."

A pane of glass shattered then, and fell splintering at her feet. She could hear a man's breath outside.

"Open the door, Ma'am," he ordered. "Colonel Brownlow is taking over this house."

"Yankees!" gasped Teresa. "Brownlow's troops."

Was this Brownlow, the old "Parson," the renegade Southerner who had taken arms against his own people? Every atrocity in the region was credited to vindictive Parson Brownlow. He was reported to have shot wounded boys on the ground, hung up women by their thumbs and incited slaves to violence and revolt.

She lit the candle. "I'd better go. They might burn down the house."

"Teresa!" Sarah almost screamed. "They'll take David. They've come for David."

She went close to the bed, the candle flame

stirred her hair. "They can't take Davie, Mother. Davie's gone—with Longstreet's army—and Stretch went with him."

Sarah collapsed on her pillow. "Oh, thank God!" she breathed.

"Lie still—and be very ill. I'm going to let them in."

Four officers in blue waited outside the door. They were very tall, and at sight of her, so small, so pretty and frightened, the two younger ones took off their hats. None was very old, she saw. This must be William Brownlow, the son of the older man called the "Parson." The son was a colonel, she had heard. The youngest man of all bowed and stepped forward.

"Lieutenant Ingalls, Ma'am. We are sorry to intrude but the colonel must have quarters in this house for a few days."

Teresa drew back and let them precede her into the house. The older three all had grim, drawn faces. They were mud-splashed, booted, worn. Outside in the darkness she could hear a confusion of moving men, tramping horses, jingling stirrups, commands.

She braced herself and faced the colonel. "My mother is very ill in that room. There are two children asleep upstairs. May I bring them down, please? I don't want them to be frightened."

"Where is your father?" demanded a red-headed captain with hard, blue eyes set too close together in a weathered face.

"He has gone to Stone's River to bring back the body of my brother who was killed there."

"Dave Hunter's her father," this officer told the colonel, "red-hot Rebel."

"Your name is Hunter?" the colonel asked.

"Yes, sir. I am Teresa."

"All your brothers in the Rebel army, I suppose?"

"One was killed and one wounded. Sheldon is with Longstreet. My little brother is upstairs. He's only ten."

"How far ahead is Longstreet?" the colonel asked.

Teresa smiled disarmingly. "As a red-hot Rebel you wouldn't expect me to give you that information, would you, sir?" she asked sweetly.

28

"Not far, sir," said Lieutenant Ingalls. "There are—er—fresh signs in the road. How many rooms here, Miss Hunter?"

"Four upstairs, but my little brother and sister are sleeping in one. I'll go waken them now. But could my mother rest, please? She has been very sick since Beau was killed. She's very frail. I'll get another candle. We haven't many left— and little oil for the lamps."

"Let the children sleep," ordered the colonel. "We'll make out. Are there blankets up there?"

"Oh, yes, sir, all the beds are ready."

"How about some coffee?" asked the red-headed captain. "The colonel hasn't eaten since morning."

"Neither have the rest of you," said the colonel.

"I'm sorry," Teresa said. "We haven't any coffee. We haven't had any for a long time."

"Blockade's tight," laughed a fourth officer, a captain who had not spoken before. "Fetch some from the commissary sergeant, Lieutenant. Where's the kitchen, Miss? I guess you've got hot water."

29

"I'm afraid the fire may be very low. We've had to save our wood too, lately. We have only one man any more and he's very sullen and lazy. I'll get the key if you'll wait, please."

Lieutenant Ingalls had gone out but the others stood waiting while she went into her mother's room and closed the door.

Sarah was sitting bolt upright, her eyes big and full of terror. Teresa pushed her down firmly, pulled the quilt up over her shoulders.

"You're very sick, remember? There are four of them, two captains, young Colonel Brownlow—not the old one, Mother, the dreadful Brownlow. They are sleeping here, so don't dare stir out of this bed, and they want to make coffee, so I'm taking the key."

"The children," whispered Sarah, taut with panic.

"Colonel Brownlow told me to leave them alone. They act like gentlemen, Mother, they do really."

"No Yankee could possibly be a gentleman. If your father were here he would never allow such an outrage of his home."

30

"If he opposed them they'd probably arrest him or he'd be shot. I'm glad he's not here. I only pray he doesn't come back till they leave."

She took the keys from her mother's basket, led the waiting men through the cistern passageway and unlocked the kitchen door. The room was dark and warm, embers glowed in the fireplace.

"My Lord, no stove!" exclaimed the quiet captain. "I'd no idea the people were so primitive down here."

"Well, we live well anyway," the redheaded captain bristled. "You Indiana fellows needn't think that all the people down here are like these Rebels."

"Our cook doesn't like stoves," Teresa explained. "She's afraid a stove would blow up in her face. She's a very good cook so we humor her."

There was kindling and lightwood piled in a corner and Teresa knelt and blew the fire to a blaze, swung the heavy iron kettle over it on the crane. The kettle was too hot to touch and soon began to steam. She set out the cups and

31

the tin spoons the servants used. No Yankee
should touch her mother's silver. Most of it,
except the little they used every day, was hidden anyway.

"Here is the coffee pot, gentlemen." She set
out the great blackened affair. "It's clean inside,
I'm sure, but it might taste of acorns or sweet
potatoes. Lizzie makes weird brews in it sometimes. Now, if you'll permit me, I'll go back to
my mother. She's badly frightened. We've never
had an army in our house before. And would
you please lock this door when you leave?"

The redheaded captain laughed too loudly
at this, and the quiet one muttered at him to
shut up. The girl was being decent enough,
wasn't she? Then the redhead gave a whoop.
Teresa turned back from the door stiff with
consternation. The redhead had discovered the
cake. Lizzie had covered it with two clean tea-
towels. It was golden, thick, and smelled de-
licious.

"Ha! Cake! They were expecting us," the
redhead cried. "Where's a knife?" He began
jerking open drawers and cupboards.

Teresa made a small sound of protest, half moan, half sob.

"The children's Christmas! All the Christmas they'll have, poor little things!"

The colonel stared at her, frowned, looked almost incredulously at the others.

"Christmas? My God—Christmas!"

"Tomorrow—or should I say today, sir?"

The redhead had found a knife and was already haggling at the cake. "You first, colonel." He held out a square hunk on the knife.

The colonel took it, tasted a crumb hungrily, stood looking first at Teresa then at the golden slice on his palm. "I'll wait for the coffee," he said awkwardly then.

"Where the devil is that lieutenant anyway?" demanded the redhead, still working on the cake.

"Please," began Teresa, timidly, "could I have one small piece—just a taste—for the children?"

"How many children?" asked Colonel Brownlow.

"Two. Drusie is nine and Gillie is ten. They wanted a Christmas tree—but we can't get one, and they strung popcorn and Lizzie baked the cake—"

"Save some cake for the children, Pressly," ordered the colonel.

"Little Rebels are as tough as big Rebels, Colonel," argued redheaded Pressly. "Remember that brat down Loudon way who turned all our horses loose?"

"But ours wouldn't—" began Teresa, then fell silent. How did she know what Gillie would do? Or even Drusie? Gillie had worn himself out the previous day pumping water for the thirsty Confederate troops. Gillie would think it a splendid thing to turn Yankee horses loose, send them stampeding over the muddy winter fields.

"Nevertheless these little Rebels get a piece of their Christmas cake," insisted the colonel. "This young lady, too. Cut a chunk for her, Captain Pressly."

"Oh, no!" choked Teresa. "I couldn't!"

"She can't eat with the Union army," sneered Pressly, coming close to her. "She'd spit on us

right now if she wasn't such a damned fine lady.
Listen, gal"—he took Teresa by the arm and
pinched hard—"I'm a neighbor of yours, know
that? I live right up yonder in Union County.
You'd like to spit on me right now, wouldn't
you, my elegant heifer? All right, here's your
cake! Now eat it, and don't turn up your nose
at good loyal Union men."

She backed away from him against the wall,
her eyes blazing, but she made no sound.

"Let that girl alone!" snapped the quiet captain.

"That will do, Pressly," said the colonel.
"We're not fighting women and children."

"She'd fight us mighty quick," protested
Pressly. "If she'd had a gun she'd have shot us
all, before ever she let us in the door."

"I have a gun," stated Teresa coldly. "My
father left it for me to protect my mother. But
I would not shoot a gentleman—even if he wore
a blue uniform."

"Better apologize, Pressly—if you wish to
continue being a gentleman," advised the quiet
captain.

Pressly shuffled his feet. "All right, Miss. I'm sorry. Now, will you eat the cake?"

"Thank you." She took the piece and held it in her hand. "I'll save it for my mother."

The door crashed back then, letting in a gust of cold air and Lieutenant Ingalls, who carried a tow sack over his shoulder.

"I had some trouble, sir, with that commissary officer. These supplies belong to the other regiment, our wagons haven't caught up yet. Coffee —but it has to be ground, and I got hardtack and some fat meat but no sugar."

"They baked a cake, they must have sugar," said Pressly.

"Could you spare us a little sugar—at least enough for the colonel's coffee, Miss?"

"I don't know how much we have," Teresa said. "I'll have to ask my mother." She started out. "She keeps the sugar locked up and gives it out every day. The coffee mill"—she pointed— "is there on the wall behind you."

"Now we hold the Mississippi there won't be any more sugar coming up the river for these snobs to put in their juleps and toddies," remarked Pressly, "but they can still bake cakes."

Teresa ignored him coolly, started out. "Better go with her, Ingalls," Pressly said. "She might lock the door or come out with that gun."

In the cistern room the lieutenant laid a delaying hand on Teresa's arm.

"Don't mind Pressly, Miss Hunter," he said. "Not all our officers are so ill bred. He comes from up in these hills somewhere. Southern Union men, as probably you know, are more vindictive and given to violence than those of us who come from the Northern states. I won't intrude on your sick mother. I'll wait outside her door. Just a little sugar, please—enough to sweeten some coffee."

A little sob caught in Teresa's throat. She had stiffened herself rigidly not to reveal even by a gesture that she resented the rudeness of the man Pressly, but the lieutenant's gentleness broke past the barrier of her control.

"It wouldn't be so bad if it weren't Christmas," she said, "and that wouldn't matter too much either, if it weren't for the children."

The lieutenant tightened his grip on her arm. "Maybe we can work out something," he said. "We're not beasts, Miss Hunter. We're men caught up in the midst of an ugly war who have to fight it out the best we can. Those men in there have all got children of their own—even Pressly's got some kids, I've heard. Colonel Brownlow isn't the hard, bitter man his old father is."

She drew away from him, made her voice crisp. "Thank you. Don't trouble about us, please. We ask only to be let alone. I'll get the sugar now."

# 3

You may as well sleep, Teresa," her mother urged, when they were alone in the room again. "Nobody knows what may happen tomorrow. They will probably turn us all out of the house. It's only three o'clock. Lie here behind me and try to rest and pray your father doesn't come."

Teresa lay down when she had built up the fire, but she could not sleep. There were men's voices in the hall, booted feet thudded on the stairs and, outside, dimly flickering through the curtains, flared the flames of bivouac fires built on the lawn.

Lizzie and Mir'am were likely shivering with terror in their cabins, the covers pulled over their heads. Maybe they would be turned out at daylight too. Light was beginning to show thinly in a hostile winter sky when the key turned, the door opened, and a bulky shadow loomed in the room. Teresa sprang up, scurried to the fireplace for the poker, but it was only Lizzie, enormously quaking.

"Miss Tess," she hissed softly. "Here you' Mamma's key. I'm a goin', Miss Tess. Them Yankees say I gotta cook for 'um, and I ain't cookin' for no folks what shot my li'l Massa Beau. Mir'am, she can cook for 'um does she love Yankee freedom so good. I'm goin' down the road. Does they git gone I come back."

"Lizzie, you can't leave us!" protested Teresa. "They'll catch you and bring you back."

"No'm, they won't. Mought be they cotch me, but they cain't lif' me and they ain't fotchin' me back long as I got my razor. You keep this door fastened good, Miss Tess. Take keer you' Mamma till I gits back."

Sarah roused, sat up. "What is it? Lizzie, the Yankees are here."

"Yes'm, I knows. They done busted in my door already. They done say I gotta cook. I tole 'um I ain't cook for no Yankee trash. My Mis'tiss, she a lady—she ain't make me cook for no white trash, no time, I tole 'um."

"Lizzie says she's running away, Mother."

"If only we could all run away! Where can you go, Lizzie?"

"I knows a place. I come back, Miss, does this trash git theyselves gone off our place." Hugely waddling, Lizzie vanished into the cold darkness outside. Teresa bolted the door but before she could lie down again bony knuckles rapped on the panels.

"Miss—Miss! Let me in. It's Mir'am."

"I suppose she's running off too," sighed Teresa as she slipped the bolt. "What is it, Mir'am? Your friends, the Yankees, are here— the ones who gave you your freedom. You mean, you aren't happy about it? Do you want to run off down the big road too, with Lizzie?"

"No'm, I ain't runnin' down no road. Them soldiers say I gotta cook. They done lef' the kitchen door open and that Lizzie, she poured two buckets full of water on the fire."

41

In spite of herself Teresa giggled. "Oh, my Heaven! What next? As though we haven't trouble enough already! Take a shovelful of coals from this grate and kindle a new fire, Mir'am, and you'd better do what those soldiers tell you to do."

"I gotta carry out all them wet ashes. I tole 'um I ain't no cook. I tole 'um I's a lady's maid, so they say they all ladies and I better git to maidin' right quick. What we goin' eat if they hog up all our vittles, Mis'tiss?"

"They have their own food. If they take ours, there's nothing we can do about it. Do what they tell you, Mir'am, and don't talk back or we all may be going down the big road," Sarah said.

"You want me fix sumpin' for Mist' Davie?"

"Davie's gone safely away. He's with the army. He'll be taken care of."

"Praise Gawd for that! Gimme that shovel, Miss Tess."

"Don't set the house on fire going through, Mir'am. I'm sure you can cook well enough for those Yankee officers."

"Lawd sakes, here's Miss Baby. Don't you joggle me, Miss Baby, or I spill this yere fire."

Drusie flew in, barefooted, big-eyed. "Mother! There's a man in Stretch's bed—and Mother, it's not Stretch."

"We have guests for Christmas, Drusie," Teresa said quickly. "Stay here with Mother and no one will hurt you."

But Drusie was trembling with excitement. "Sis, I saw his coat! It was a blue coat with gold on it! It's Yankees! Mean, stinky old Yankees in Stretch's bed."

"Yes dear, they are Yankee officers," Sarah said. "We didn't invite them but we have to be polite to them even if we hate them."

"When Father comes he'll shoot them all dead! He will, won't he? He'll shoot that man in Stretch's bed and there'll be blood all over everything."

"Oh, God!" moaned Sarah, prayerfully. "My children—my little girl, to live through times like this!"

"They aren't bad Yankees, Drusie," declared

Teresa. "They are just men and they have little girls too. Little girls like you."

"They're devils, anyway," stated Drusie viciously, "and their little girls are little devil girls, too. Mother,"—panic whitened her face— "they'll get Davie!"

"No, Drusie. We sent Davie away. Davie is safe."

Drusie wriggled into the bed. "That's a joke on the Yankees, anyway. And we won't have to crawl up in the cold, dark attic any more."

Teresa lay down again and it was broad daylight when awareness came to her. The sun was streaming in at the curtains, a bugle was blowing outside and someone was knocking on the door. Her mother was sleeping again too, so she tiptoed around the bed and with Drusie, curious, at her heels she opened the door a cautious crack.

Lieutenant Ingalls stood there, and behind him was Mir'am, carrying a big tray loaded with dishes.

"Breakfast," announced the lieutenant with a

44

smile. "Your cook has taken herself off, but this woman did the best she could. Please accept this with the compliments of the regiment, Ma'am, and I wish you a not-too-unhappy Christmas."

Drusie stared and stiffened. "Christmas!" she cried. "Mir'am, don't you dare let the Yankees eat our cake."

Mir'am shrugged sadly. "They done et it a'ready, Miss Baby. All but a little smidgy piece for you and Mast' Gillie."

"Why, you stealers, you mean, mean robbers!" Drusie flew at the lieutenant, tears streaming down her face, and before Teresa could restrain her, she was kicking him savagely in the shins with her little bare toes. "I hate you! I hate you!" she shrilled. "I'll tell my daddy to kill you all dead!"

Teresa pulled the child away and Drusie flung herself on the bed and burst into wild sobbing.

"I'm sorry, Lieutenant," Teresa said. "They had counted so much on that cake."

"Don't apologize for the little girl. It's we

45

who should be sorry. I did try to make up a little for the cake. I went out up the lane early this morning and cut a little Christmas tree. If you'll tell me where you'd like it set up—"

"If you will refrain from annoying us, that is all we ask," said Sarah stonily.

Drusie sprang up hot-eyed. "I hope you all get an awful belly ache, eating our Christmas cake!" she cried, "and I don't want your old Christmas tree. If you bring it in here I'll kick it down. I'll set fire to it and burn it up!"

The lieutenant smiled ruefully, turned, and walked away.

"That was rude, Drusie," reproved Teresa. "Soldiers have to do what they're ordered to do —and it was kind of the lieutenant to fetch you a Christmas tree. Shall we put it up in the dining room? You can string the popcorn to trim it."

"Nobody ordered them to eat our cake," pouted Drusie, unmollified.

"They got vittles, anyway," Mir'am remarked. "Y'all better eat while you got a chance."

46

"Our food, I suppose?" snapped Sarah.

"No'm, it ain't. They fotch it up in tow sacks outen them wagons, got coffee too."

"It smells good," admitted Drusie, reluctantly. "Biscuits and bacon and coffee."

Sarah frowned, white-faced. "Surely, Teresa, you're not going to eat that food? Food from our enemies, from the assassins who killed your brother?"

Teresa set her chin. "I'm going to eat it, and so are you, Mother. Why shouldn't we eat it when it's offered graciously? Probably we won't be allowed in our own kitchen anyway, if there's anything left there to cook. And there may not be, if they've raided the smokehouse and the cellar."

"I shall not eat it, I'd starve first. I couldn't swallow it, I'd choke."

"Maybe they put poison in it," suggested Drusie, sniffing at the dishes. "It doesn't smell like poison—not like what Lanus puts out to kill the rats."

"Mother, at least drink a little coffee."

"No—no, don't ask me. Mir'am, when you get

47

a chance make me a pot of strong tea. We do have tea, don't we?"

"Mought be I could scrape a few crumbs outen the jar. I fix it."

"Lock the door again, Teresa," Sarah said, when Mir'am had gone out.

"Gillie will be hungry." Drusie bit into a biscuit. "I don't believe this is poisoned. Anyway it would be quicker to kill us with swords or shoot us, wouldn't it?"

"They don't kill women and children, Drusie," Teresa said. "They kill only enemy soldiers."

"No," wailed Sarah, "they don't kill women, they just torture them to death!"

"Mother, please! You're frightening Drusie. And today is Christmas."

"Christmas!" Distilled bitterness crackled in her mother's voice. "Let's not speak the word again. Christ would refuse to be born into a world like this. God has forgotten us and no one could blame Him."

"Gillie got up early." Drusie polished off another biscuit stuffed with bacon. "His

48

pants and shoes were gone when I came
down."

"I'd better tell Mir'am to look for him then."
Teresa put down her cup. The coffee had been
hot and strong, so wonderfully good after being
without any so long.

"Teresa, you're not going out of this room!"
cried Sarah. "Not with those ruffians in the
house. I won't allow it."

Teresa gave an impatient shrug. "Oh, Mother,
I was in the kitchen an hour with those officers
last night. They were all very decent—all but
one captain, named Pressly. And he wasn't a
Yankee at all, he said he came from up in Union
County."

"This country is full of Presslys. Some of them
are good people, but they never owned any
Negroes. There was a man named Pressly who
bought a horse from your father once. He
brought it back later and claimed it was blind
in one eye. But your father always insisted that
this Pressly had blinded the horse after he
bought it by beating it over the head."

"Maybe it's the same man. He was very scorn-

49

ful when he spoke of Father. He was very scorn-
ful of everything."

"And you'd go out and risk being insulted
by a man like that? Why don't they go on
about their business? They're supposed to be
fighting a war, not enjoying a holiday in this
house."

"I'm not going to be intimidated by Captain Pressly or any other Yankee soldier," said
Teresa stoutly. "I'll go up and fetch your
clothes, Drusie. You'll catch cold in your night
wrapper and bare feet."

She found Gillespie in the kitchen absorbedly
watching a very dirty sergeant who was taking
a gun to pieces on the table, wiping all the
parts on one of Lizzie's dish towels. The sergeant looked at her and grunted, but Gillie did
not even look up. She had to give him a sharp
command twice before he stirred and reluctantly followed her out to the cistern room.
There he pulled back and faced her stub-
bornly.

"You leave me be!" he muttered. "You know
what I'm going to do? I'm going to wait till he

50

gets that gun cleaned and loaded and then I'll watch where he puts it and I'll get it and kill me a Yankee."

She shook him hard. "Gillie, you shall not! You stay away from them, you hear me? You shoot at one Yankee and they'd burn this house down and us in it. Mother wants you now, so come along and hush."

"You know what they did? They ate most all our cake. Mir'am gave me one little smidgy piece. And they killed all our hens and now they're out there stealing all the corn in the crib, Mir'am said so. If Father was here he'd shoot them mighty quick."

"Father mustn't come back—not now. I wish we had someone to send down the road to head him off. Did you see Lanus anywhere, Gillie?"

"He's run off. Lizzie ran off too. Mir'am says she's going to run off and be free, if it stops raining."

"Raining? But the sun was out just a little while ago."

"Well, it's raining now."

She listened, heard rain falling steadily, doggedly, on the roof of the cistern house and water was running melodiously into the cistern. Outside, she could see through the latticed walls that all the little fires were out and men were huddling like cold dogs in the porch and under the wagons.

"They aren't going to march today because it's raining," Gillie went on. "That soldier said so. All their wagons would get stuck and anyway he knows where Longstreet's camped out, he says, and they can go up there and lick him any time they get ready. The colonel is half sick and all worn out, that soldier says, so they're letting him sleep today. Then he won't make 'em march in the rain."

"They're very confident, I suppose, that Longstreet won't turn and come back and capture them all?" Teresa remarked.

"Oh, they say he got the tar beat out of him down the road. He can't fight any more, they say, till he gets some more men and more guns. If Stretch knew they were here I reckon he'd ride up to General Longstreet's tent and tell

him to come back and run 'em off our place.
Longstreet could lick 'em easy this morning,
half of 'em asleep and the rest half drunk and
the horses gone lame, most of 'em."

They passed the dining room and Gillie
stopped and stared. "Jeerusalem! A Christmas
tree! Did Lanus come back?"

"No, Lieutenant Ingalls brought it in. He's
got it nailed to a board too. You and Drusie can
put popcorn strings on it, anyway, Gillie."

"What you doin', Yank?" demanded Gillie
abruptly, harshly.

Captain Pressly emerged from behind the
little green tree. He held out a hand, in which
were three bright, shining brass buttons.

"Tryin' to make these stick on the branches,"
he said, half shamefaced. "Thought they might
shine up a little. Been carryin' 'em around for a
long time—buttons always busting off in
battles."

"Thank you, Captain. That is very thoughtful
of you," Teresa said. "Come along Gillie,
Mother's worrying about you."

They went into Sarah's room and Sarah

53

clutched her young son and held him tight. "You're all the man I've got now, Gillespie!"

"Yes'm." Gillie shrugged free, uncomfortably embarrassed. "I reckon that means I get to carry in all the wood. I wisht I could shoot me one Yankee, though. I won't never get such a good chance again."

"Huh!" Drusie looked up from struggling with the buttons on her shoes. "You wouldn't even know which end of the gun to shoot! Lanus showed you that time and you let the gun kick you clear across the barn lot."

"It did not! It only kicked me a little piece, Miss Smarty. Anyway, the load was too heavy, Lanus said so."

"That's enough, children. Gillie, eat your breakfast."

"Oh, cracky! Bacon! I wonder where they stole that from? Some place down the road, I bet."

The morning wore on. A muddy private knocked on the door with an armful of wood, but Sarah would not let him come in. Grumbling, loudly, Gillie carried it in from the hall.

"Fence posts," he announced. "Here's some wire and staples hanging to this piece."

"I reckon they'll burn the barn down next," observed Drusie, curled on the hearth. "Did you taste of that cake, Gillie?"

"One taste. It was just fair." He battled the fire with the poker.

"Why don't you string your popcorn?" asked Teresa. "It will be something to do."

"Huh!" scorned Gillie. "Oh—all right. I wisht it would snow. Snow about four feet deep and bury those ole Yankees."

"It would snow on Davie too. Here's a needle. Wash your hands first, and you'd better fill the pitcher too, Gillie. Be sure to cover the cistern afterwards."

"They left the cover off all day. I bet they pumped about all the water out of it too, they watered a thousand horses, almost."

"It's raining, fortunately. All the cisterns will soon fill up if it keeps on like this."

Drusie had declined to be interested in the popcorn stringing. She stood at the windows, watching what went on outside, now and then turning to report.

"There goes that lieutenant riding off. He's got two soldiers with him."

"Maybe they're going after Longstreet." Gillie rushed to the window, trailing popcorn across the carpet. "They'd better not shoot Stretch and Davie."

Sarah, who had returned to her bed, began to sob again. Drusie turned on her sharply.

"You promised not to cry on Christmas! You said no tears on Christmas, Mamma—you did, you did!"

"Hush, darling, you mustn't talk to Mother that way!"

"Well, she did promise!"

"I know, dear," said Sarah, wiping her eyes. "I'll try to remember."

The morning dragged. The clouds thickened and it grew very gloomy, and the rain fell faster. Cold crept in through the walls and fretful gusts of wind set smoke flicking out into the room from the smoldering logs on the fire.

At noon Mir'am came with a tray. "Nothing

but peas," she said, disgustedly, as she bumped it down on the table. "Got some meat in 'um though, and I cooked some bread."

"Are the Yankees getting ready to leave, Mir'am?" Teresa asked. "We saw some of them ride away."

"Them fellers just went to town. They ain't tole me nothin'. Come in and borry my fire till I ain't got enough to cook with scarcely, they all mighty cold and mis'able, I knows that."

"We could sing," suggested Teresa, when they had coaxed their mother to eat a little of Mir'am's hot bread. "You start, Mother, let's sing *Silent Night*."

"Oh, no! Oh, Teresa, how could you—carols on a day like this!"

"Drusie and I will sing then. Come on, Drusie. '*God rest ye, merry gentlemen—*'"

"'*Let nothing you dismay,*'" piped Drusie. Then Gillespie gave a yell from the window.

"Horses! In our cornfield. Cavalry! Confederate cavalry!"

# 4

THERE were sudden yells outside. Shots and running feet. Men charged into the hall, shouting, slamming doors. Teresa flew to the window. A small troop of gray-clad men were riding into the yard, firing as they came. Bullets pinged against the chimney, a window splintered above her head and she dropped to her knees as the glass showered down.

"Down! Get down!" she screamed at the excited children. But Gillie was dancing up and down at the window.

"Yay! Looky them Yankees run! Yi-eee—e!"

The horses pounded around the house. There was a fusillade of shots and more glass crashed. Upstairs, shots were being fired from the windows.

"Gillie—get down! Lie flat on the floor!"

ordered Sarah, who had slipped out of bed and crouched, huddled in a blanket, with Drusie pressed close against her. But Gillie was deaf and oblivious with excitement. He knelt, shouting encouragement to the galloping troops, who came swinging back again, to fire at the fleeing Union soldiers. A horse broke loose, plunged across the porch, smashing the railing. From the kitchen Teresa could hear Mir'am's shrill repeated screaming.

"They're after Brownlow—I hope they come in and get him," yelled Gillie, pounding his fists on the windowsill. But the cavalry did not dismount. They fired another round at the men about the house, then wheeled and pounded off across the corn stubble.

The firing from the house abruptly ceased. Teresa crept on her knees to the window to see the gray troop vanishing in the rain, one man leading a riderless horse. In the muddy yard three men in blue lay prone rain beating on their bodies. Teresa shut her eyes and swallowed hard, looking away.

"They got a few of 'em anyway," gloated

Gillie. "Looky—they got an officer. They're carrying them in. It's that lieutenant, by cracky!"

Teresa caught her breath, stood up, broken glass crunching under her feet. Up the drive three soldiers in blue were carrying Lieutenant Ingalls, whose boots dangled. One arm hung limply, dripping blood; in the other arm he clutched tightly a soggy, paper-wrapped parcel.

"Lieutenant Ingalls—they shot him!" Teresa gasped.

"Teresa, you shan't go out there!" ordered Sarah sharply, getting to her feet and spilling Drusie on the floor. "You come back, you hear?"

"No—no he's wounded. He's hurt." Teresa was out in the hall in a breath, pushing through the confused crowd of wet, muddy men who smelled of powder and gunsmoke. She tore the back door open and let the bearers enter, aware of Gillie staring behind her, of Colonel Brownlow plunging down the stairs coatless, smoke-blackened, and towsled.

"Fetch a mattress!" the colonel was yelling to the men above him.

"In here," Teresa opened the door of the dining room. They carried Lieutenant Ingalls in, and Teresa touched his cold hand. He gave her a wan, bloodless smile.

"Christmas gift," he said, "Christmas gift from Vaughan's cavalry."

Mattresses came tumbling down the stairs and Teresa stripped the day cloth from the dining room table swiftly. "Here," she directed the panting men who carried the lieutenant. "A mattress first—now, lay him here."

Brownlow was shouting. "Rouse up Captain Pugh. Get him down here."

"He's drunk, sir. He never heard the fighting," reported a little corporal.

"Throw some water on him. There are men down here needing surgery. Get some sheets— towels—" He turned on Teresa his eyes harsh and impatient, "Get us some stuff for bandages," he directed, "and hot water—plenty of hot water."

Teresa ran to her mother's room, jerked the sheet from the bed ignoring Sarah's outraged eyes. Drusie came running out too and stood staring at the wounded officer on the dining room table. The lieutenant managed a sick grin at her. "Poor shots, weren't they, little sister? They didn't kill me."

"It serves you right," said Drusie solemnly "for eating up our Christmas cake."

"But I never got a crumb of your cake, not one solitary crumb."

Drusie's lip quivered at the sight of the dripping blood. "I'll give you mine, then, if no Yankee ate it up yet," she promised impulsively.

"There are four men outside, wounded and still alive, Colonel," reported a soldier, easing the damp bundle out of Lieutenant Ingalls' grasp.

"What's that anyway?" demanded the colonel, as the soldier laid the parcel down gingerly.

"Mine, Colonel," said Ingalls. "A little Christmas."

"Too damn' much Christmas around here now! Bring those wounded men in, you men! Don't stand there gawking. Where the hell is that doctor, anyway?"

"I woke him, Colonel. He's still groggy."

"Get him down here on the double. There are men that need surgery immediately. All of you stand back and give this lieutenant air."

There was air to spare pouring down the stairway from the open windows above. Wet, raw gusts blew in at the open door and there were rain stains and blood stains on the carpets. Teresa was ripping the sheet into strips, tearing at it with fingers and teeth. The quiet captain took the bandages from her, bent over the lieutenant.

"Clean through," he said, "missed his heart. You're lucky, fellow."

"Where the devil is Pugh? Why don't he get down here?"

"Here he comes, Colonel."

A blear-eyed man in an undershirt and rumpled trousers was stumbling down the stairs. His face was flushed and swollen, his hands shook. Behind him the corporal carried a leather instrument case.

"Stand back," yelled the corporal importantly. "Give the doctor room."

Men came running from the kitchen with steaming pots of water. Other men grunted in carrying the soaked, groaning wounded men from the yard. These they laid on the mattresses on the floor, sponged their faces, eased their bleeding legs and arms. Soldiers jerked open drawers, dragging out Sarah's linen napkins to stanch the blood.

"Light," shouted Captain Pugh, bending over the lieutenant, "candles—lamps—expect me to work in the dark?"

Candles appeared quickly, their few precious candles. Mir'am stuck her head in at the door.

"You-all want water b'ilin', you better send somebody to fotch me some wood."

The colonel jerked an imperative thumb. "You there—'tend to that wood detail. Listen, Miss"—he fixed Teresa with a stony eye—"this is no place for a young lady. I advise you to return to your mother."

"No—no, I want to help," she protested. "I can help. I'm not afraid."

The doctor turned and snapped at her. "Girl—

64

hold a finger here—on this artery, till I get it tied off. Her hands are smaller," he explained to the colonel.

They had cut away the lieutenant's coat and it lay in a sodden mass under him. Teresa bent over and pressed hard on the torn and leaping blood vessel, as the surgeon directed, her heart pounding, sick hot water surging up into her mouth. But she made herself stand steadily, and the lieutenant lay very still, though beads of perspiration stood out on his face. Someone with big red, dirty hands was wiping them off, and Teresa looked up into the face of Captain Pressly.

He gave her a one-sided smile. "You've got courage, Miss Hunter," he said. "Not many gals could take a bloody job like that."

"My brother was wounded," she reminded him. "I had to dress his wound every day."

"Reckon people are all alike, when it's trouble," Pressly observed, sponging away blood. "I didn't mean what I said, out yonder in the kitchen. About you bein' a snob—things like that."

65

"It's all right," said Teresa.

Captain Pugh's whisky breath blew hot in her face but he knotted the catgut swiftly, and the surge of blood was stopped.

"You can get back now, Miss," he said. "You were damn' lucky, Lieutenant. He'll be all right now, if he don't get any gangrene or lung fever."

"Oh, he won't. I'll take care of him," insisted Teresa.

"I was lucky," Lieutenant Ingalls managed a wan grin, reached his good hand and gave Teresa's icy fingers a pat.

For no reason at all, she trembled with foolish happiness. These men were enemies. They were part of that remorseless juggernaut that was crushing the South, the relentless force that had killed Beau and wounded Davie, who would destroy this house if they chose, and make her father a prisoner. She should rejoice in their calamity, in their miseries, she should be full of hate instead of this odd tenderness that moved her to bend and wipe cold dew from the lieutenant's face gently, and then to sponge

66

another man's muddy face and hold water to the thin, shaking lips of a third.

Her dress was drabbled and stained, her fingers were numb with cold. Her head felt queerly light as though this was not her body at all but some light husk of a woman made of air, moved by the will of a stubborn spirit.

They were enemies, but also they were men, caught up in the cruel machine of war, stripped of their identity, stripped of their own wills, made into machines for murder, automatic and insensate in destruction. Now the metal of that ruthlessness was shattered, their flesh bared and torn by the common humanity of pain. Even Gillie had ceased to grin, triumphantly, he was on his knees before the fire in the grate that some soldiers had kindled, blowing hard on a lighted splinter of wood.

Teresa saw her mother then, stood still and amazed. Sarah was fully dressed, she had come quietly into the room and stood regarding the confusion and bloody mess with shocked and pitying eyes. Teresa ran to her and turned her around.

"Mother—no! You must not be here. You must go back to bed."

But Sarah put her off calmly. "These men should have beds," she said. "You may have them carried upstairs, Colonel."

The colonel bowed, awful weariness in his eyes, the sick weariness of war.

"Thank you, Ma'am, but they will do better where they are. We'll put the lieutenant on the floor so he won't ruin your table. But these hurt men will have to remain here, Ma'am, even after we move on. I'll leave a detail to take care of them, of course, I'll see that your house is not molested—not by our men, at any rate. For your Rebel boys, I can't promise."

"You had best leave some food for them also, Colonel," Sarah said. "Since two armies have passed over this place, I fear we have very little left."

"I'll give an order to the commissary, Ma'am. Just one question—did you send that big Negro woman out to fetch Vaughan's troop down on us?"

Sarah drew herself up. "I did not, sir! Though

I assure you that if I had known that Vaughan was in the neighborhood, I should very likely have done it. Wouldn't you expect me to have done it, Colonel Brownlow?"

He grinned thinly. "I should certainly have expected you to do exactly that, Mrs. Hunter. However, I take your word that you had no part in it. You wouldn't be offering aid and comfort to my men if you had conspired at their deaths, anyway I'll assume that. But I could not have blamed you, if you had planned to have us taken. This is an unhappy war, Ma'am. Unhappy for all of us."

He bowed again and strode away. They heard him barking orders in the hall. Lieutenant Ingalls was eased gently down to a pallet on the floor, and when he was made comfortable, he gestured with a pale hand.

"Over there—that bundle," he whispered to Teresa.

"Not now," objected the surgeon, "I've just give him an opium pill. He needs to rest."

"Now," insisted the lieutenant.

Teresa brought the parcel, the wrapping wet and torn.

"I had a hard time finding anything in that little town to the west," he said. "They didn't like Yankees, but when I showed the man some hard money he sold me those little trinkets. I wanted the little girl to have her Christmas— even if the Yankees did eat her cake. Open it, Miss Hunter."

Teresa broke the damp strings, unrolled the soggy newspapers in which it had been wrapped. There was a small doll in the package, with yellow painted curls and a sodden pink dress. There was a knife for Gillie, and two china cups and saucers, one cup with a handle broken and a smear of blood upon it.

"Best I could do," gasped Ingalls, drowsily, "for you all—Christmas."

Tears ran down Teresa's cheeks, as she looked up at her mother. On an impulse she bent and kissed the lieutenant's drained face.

"They won't—move me—yet," he whispered, as he slipped into merciful unconsciousness.

"No, they won't move you yet," she answered. "I'll take care of you. And some day the war will be over."

"I'll come back," the whisper was so faint she could hardly catch it, "Sing—sing for Christmas!"

"Drusie!" Teresa pulled the little girl down beside her on the stained carpet, "Sing Drusie— my throat hurts—"

Drusie's small voice piped out, shrilly. Teresa tried to sing, but the pain was too sharp. Tears came instead.

*"For Jesus, Christ our Saviour, was born on Christmas day,"* warbled the little girl,

*"Now to the Lord sing praises, all ye within this place,*
*"And with true love and brotherhood each other now embrace.*
*"This holy tide of Christmas doth bring re-deeming grace."*

A deeper voice had joined in and Teresa looked up into the misted eyes and flushed face of Captain Pressly. He was singing at the top of his voice, and tears were running down his cheeks.

Then from the door, where she had lingered, they heard Sarah Hunter say, softly, "God bless us, every one!"

# TENDER

Freed

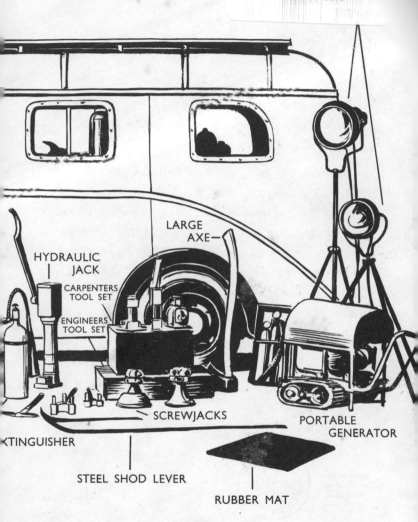

LARGE
AXE

HYDRAULIC
JACK

CARPENTERS
TOOL SET

ENGINEERS
TOOL SET

SCREWJACKS

PORTABLE
GENERATOR

XTINGUISHER

STEEL SHOD LEVER

RUBBER MAT

Series 606B

*Here is a carefully planned reference book which will help to answer the many questions that lively children ask.*

*Interesting and accurate information about the Fire Service is given within the limits of a relatively simple vocabulary. Even children whose reading experience is limited will be encouraged by the carefully prepared text and magnificent illustrations to find out for themselves about this essential Service, and at the same time gain extra reading practice.*

**A LADYBIRD
EASY-READING
BOOK**

~~2/6~~
NET

LADYBIRD
**15p**
NET
REVISED PRICE

A LADYBIRD 'EASY-READING' BOOK

'People at work'
# THE FIREMAN

*by*
VERA SOUTHGATE, M.A., B.Com.
*and* J. HAVENHAND

*with illustrations by*
JOHN BERRY

Publishers: Wills & Hepworth Ltd., Loughborough
*First published 1962* &copy; *Printed in England*

# THE FIREMAN

You have often seen a fire engine rushing along the road, with its bells ringing. Cars, lorries and buses move to the side of the road, to make way for the fire engine.

The firemen must get to the fire as quickly as possible, in case people are in danger. If the firemen arrive in time they can stop small fires growing into large ones.

7214 0062 0

All fire engines are painted bright red. There are different kinds of engines, which are used for different sorts of fires.

The smallest engine is called a Pump Tender. It carries two hundred gallons of water in its tank.

A larger fire engine is called a Pump Water Tender. It carries four hundred gallons of water. This engine is used where there is no water supply near the fire.

The biggest fire engine in a fire station is called a Turntable Ladder.

The ladder on this engine can reach far higher than any of the ladders on the other fire engines. It is fixed to a special kind of table, which can be turned in any direction.

The Turntable Ladder is sent out to fires in high buildings, because its ladder will reach right to the top. It is often used to rescue people from very high buildings.

Another kind of engine is called a Salvage Tender.

At a big fire, it is not only the fire itself which causes damage. The water, which the firemen use to put out the fire, can also do a lot of damage.

The crew of the Salvage Tender protect the furniture and carpets in a house, by covering them with canvas sheets. In a factory they cover the machinery with canvas sheets to protect it.

There are usually five men in the crew of a fire engine. One of them drives the engine.

The leader sits beside the driver. The other firemen sit inside the cab of the fire engine.

The leader has usually been in the Fire Service for many years. He will know how to fight different sorts of fires. So, when the firemen arrive at a fire, it is always the leader who decides how to fight the fire. He tells each fireman what to do.

Every morning, as the firemen come on duty, each fireman is told which is his fire engine for the day.

Each fireman then puts his clothing and equipment in his own place, inside his engine. This is done in a special way, to help him to get dressed quickly for a fire.

First he folds his jacket and lays it on the seat. On top of the jacket he places his helmet. He stands his tall boots on the floor and folds the tops down.

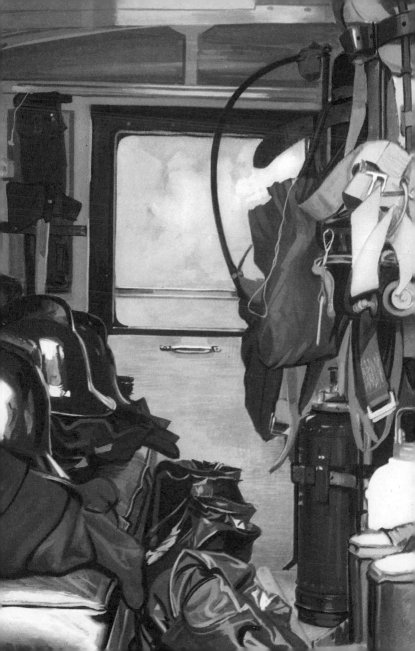

When he is called to a fire, a fireman must put his helmet on first. This is important, because it will protect his head at a fire.

A fireman's long rubber boots come right up his legs and fasten on to his trouser belt. Some firemen wear long leggings on top of strong boots. Their boots or leggings protect them from the water.

When a fireman puts on his jacket, his axe is already hooked to the belt of his jacket.

A fireman's axe is important to him, because at a fire he may need to break down a door, or chop away burning wood.

The firemen finish dressing, in the cab, as the fire engine is on its way to the fire. By the time the fire engine arrives at the fire, the firemen will be dressed and ready to fight the fire.

The picture shows a fireman who is fully dressed.

Anyone who discovers a fire should hurry to the nearest telephone and dial 999. This is called an emergency telephone call and it can be made without using any money.

The operator at the telephone exchange always answers an emergency call immediately. When the call is about a fire, the telephone operator puts the call straight through to the fire station.

In the control room at the fire station there are always people on duty, night and day. One person sits at the table near the telephone.

As soon as a fire is reported, the duty officer presses a button. This rings the alarm bells in the fire station.

The officer at the telephone makes sure that the person reporting the fire gives the correct address.

As soon as the duty officer in the control room rings the alarm bells, he must decide how many engines he will send to the fire. He must also decide which sort of engines to send.

When the engines have left the fire station, the leader can keep in touch with the fire station by radio. The radio operator, at the fire station, is sometimes a girl.

As soon as the alarm bells sound, the firemen stop whatever they are doing and run to their engines.

The firemen who are upstairs slide down a polished pole in one corner. This pole comes through a hole in the ceiling, down to the big room where the fire engines stand ready.

The drivers of the engines which are going out start their engines. The men jump in and put on their uniforms.

The leader of the crew runs into the control room. He picks up the piece of paper telling him the address of the fire.

Meanwhile the big doors in front of the fire engine have been opened.

Thirty seconds after the alarm has sounded, the engine is being driven out of the fire station, with its bells ringing.

Many of the calls are for chimney fires. Usually it does not take the firemen long to put out a chimney fire.

Many chimney fires are put out from inside the house, with a stirrup hand pump and chimney rods.

Sometimes the firemen have to use their ladders to climb on to the roof. Then they carry hoses up the ladders and send a fine spray of water down the chimney.

When a fire is put out, the fire engine goes back to the fire station.

There it is cleaned and polished. Everything is checked and put ready for the next fire.

The firemen take the wet hoses from the fire engine and hang them on tall drying towers. Then they put other dry hoses ready in the fire engine.

A fireman does not spend all his time fighting fires. Most of his time is spent at the fire station. There he has many jobs to do.

The fire engine must be kept in good running order. The fireman's equipment must always be ready for use.

Often the firemen practise climbing ladders to see how quickly they can do it. They also practise with hoses and with new equipment.

Fires often break out during the night, so firemen are on duty all night at every fire station.

Fires which break out at night are usually bigger than fires during the day. This is because people are asleep, so the fire is often not discovered until it is blazing.

People who are asleep in bed may be trapped upstairs. Then the firemen will rescue them.

At a very large fire, all the fire engines from one station are needed. Sometimes extra fire engines are brought from other towns.

Then dozens of firemen all play their hoses on to the fire.

The Chief Officer of the fire service is there. He sits in a big van called the control unit. It is fitted with radio. The Chief Officer decides how to fight the fire and how to use the engines.

Usually firemen fight fires with water from fire hydrants. Under the ground there is a pipe which brings water to our homes. Firemen can get water from this pipe at a fire hydrant. Fire hydrants are marked at the roadside with the letter H.

At fires in the country, firemen use water from a pond or stream. They throw a pipe into the pond. The fire engine then takes water out of the pond, and pumps it along the hose.

Most fires can be put out with water, but water is of no use when oil or petrol is on fire.

This is because, when oil and water are mixed, the oil always floats on top of the water. When water is poured on to burning oil and petrol, they go on burning as they float on top of the water.

If fire breaks out in an oil-tanker, or an aeroplane, firemen use a special kind of foam to fight it. This foam smothers the flames.

At some fires there is a lot of smoke. This makes it difficult for the firemen to breathe. So, the firemen who go into smoke-filled buildings must wear breathing apparatus.

Sometimes they carry small bells or walkie-talkie radios. Then they can keep in touch with one another.

If it is dark inside a building, the firemen will use their powerful hand lamps.

Firemen have other special equipment, which they use for different kinds of fires.

Often, in the country, in summer, dry grass and bushes are set on fire. When the firemen have poured water on the flames, the dead bushes still smoulder. If they are left to smoulder, they may burst into flames later.

The firemen use special beaters to beat the smouldering roots. These beaters are made of canvas flaps, fixed to wooden handles.

Firemen do not always use fire engines to fight fires. Sometimes they use fire boats on the rivers. In London there are fire boats on the river Thames.

These fire boats are painted bright red, the same as fire engines. They carry hoses and other equipment just like fire engines.

Fire boats are used to fight fires which break out in ships on the river. They can also be used, sometimes, when buildings near the banks of rivers are on fire.

The Fire Service is not only used to fight fires. Firemen often help with other jobs, where their long ladders or their pumps will be useful.

Firemen pump water out of flooded buildings. They bring down cats from trees. They pull up animals which have fallen into wells. They rescue people who have got stuck, or hurt, on roofs or ledges.

A fireman does all sorts of unusual jobs, as well as his main work of fighting fires.

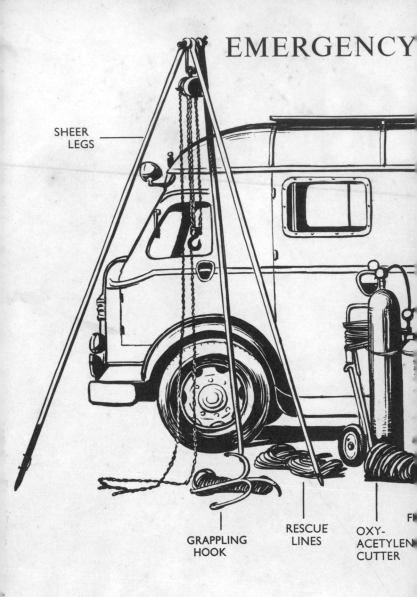

EMERGENCY

SHEER
LEGS

GRAPPLING
HOOK

RESCUE
LINES

OXY-
ACETYLEN
CUTTER